UNDER ONE

RAINBOW

words by **CHRIS AYALA-KRONOS**
pictures by **SOL SALINAS**

Clarion Books
AN IMPRINT OF HARPERCOLLINSPUBLISHERS

On Pride . . .

we express ourselves

in a rainbow of colors

with style and grace.

We laugh,

share stories, and wave flags

on the way to the parade.

Some bike. Others roll.
We walk and skip!

We dance our way through the crowd.

Our hearts feel full of love

as we move to the beats

pumping into the air.

With each step forward, we marvel at our magnificent community.

Until the sun
shines on us,
and we all
shine back.

On Pride . . .
we celebrate each other,
just as we are . . .

To those who paved the way,
to my brilliant community,
and to you, just as you are —C.A-K.

For Fraizer, Steph, and Mary,
I love existing under the same
rainbow with you. —S.S.